A Polar Bear Journey

by **Debbie S. Miller** ❄ Pictures by **Jon Van Zyle**

For Kate and Tom and their two cubs, Jack and Matthew

With special thanks to Steve Amstrup, Gerald Garner,
Craig George, and Dick Shideler for their research assistance and
to the Alaska State Council on the Arts —D. M.

For Dennis Corrington, a true friend for
more than twenty years

We've journeyed a lot of trail together . . . may the
wind be always at your back. —J. V.Z.

Little, Brown and Company
Boston New York Toronto London

Through gusting wind and swirling snow, a great white bear lumbers across the sea ice. She is pregnant and searching for a place to build her winter den.

On this frigid November day, the arctic wind plasters her fur with snow. Protected by the four inches of fat beneath her thick white coat, she reaches the ice-locked shore of the Beaufort Sea. She climbs up to the tundra and strides over to a high river bluff. The Inupiat Eskimos call this frozen waterway the Katakturuk, "the river where you can see a long way."

The bear can't see far through the blizzard, but she does spot a large snowdrift sheltered by the bluff. It is the perfect spot for a den. With her huge paws, she tunnels out a long, narrow entrance, then carves out a room the size of a big doghouse. The den is slightly higher than the tunnel, so the rising warm air is trapped inside. This will be a cozy place to give birth.

She stands on her hind legs outside the den, sniffing the air around her. Three years ago, she ran from another den site when a helicopter scared her. This year, she smells the distant bowhead whale carcass she scavenged upon recently, but there is no scent of humans or their loud machines. Satisfied, she crawls back into her new home and falls into a deep sleep.

In early January, while a sub-zero blizzard rages outside the den, the dozing bear feels movement within her body. Her heart rate increases. She pants steamy breath into the dark den. Suddenly there is a squealing sound. Then another. Two cubs are born into a frozen world without sunshine.

The helpless brother and sister each weigh about one pound. They can't see or hear yet because those senses won't develop fully for several weeks. But they can feel their mother's warmth as she licks them clean. Their tiny, sharp claws cling to her six-hundred-pound body. With the help of her guiding paws, they suckle her rich milk, then curl up and fall asleep.

When the cubs are two months old, they begin to walk and explore their snug home.
They scrape out new tunnels and smaller rooms that connect to the main den. One day
as they wrestle on the slippery floor, a faint bluish light filters through the snowy roof.
Outside, the sun is peeking over the mountains, casting its rays on the windswept fur of
some musk oxen passing by.

In late March, it becomes too warm inside the den. The mother bear claws at the icy walls and roof, which allows more oxygen to reach them. Finally she crawls down the tunnel. Her massive head bursts through the layer of snow covering the entrance, frightening a flock of ptarmigan.

She rolls and stretches, nibbles on some old berries, and takes a few mouthfuls of snow. Then she hears the cubs whimpering. She huffs to them.

Two faces hesitantly peer out of the tunnel. This is the first time they have seen the outside world. The chilling air and blinding light startle them. They spend only a short time outside before diving back into their familiar den.

Each day that follows, the cubs stay outside a little longer. One cub sniffs at a hole in the snow where lemmings are burrowing, while the other looks up at a cawing raven. The playful cubs climb up the snowdrift, then slide down on their bellies. They run, tumble, and chase each other. Every movement helps develop their muscles and coordination.

The cubs now weigh thirty pounds each, but the mother bear is thin and hungry. She has lost nearly three hundred pounds since November. On a warm April day, she leads them away from the den for good. It is time to begin their journey across the sea ice in search of food.

The polar bears are well adapted to life in the Arctic. Paws the size of dinner plates help distribute the mother's massive weight and keep her from crashing through thin ice into the frigid water. The paws are insulated with fur, and the pads are covered with tiny bumps that provide good walking traction. Although her fur looks white, it is actually made up of transparent, hollow hairs that trap the sun's warmth. Beneath the fur is black skin, which absorbs the heat. Like insulation, her thick layers of fat and fur prevent the heat from escaping.

The cubs stay in their mother's tracks, running to keep up with her long strides. Sometimes they climb onto her back for a free ride. When they are tired and hungry, she sits in the snow and nurses them.

The mother bear climbs over a pressure ridge, where the wind and ocean currents have piled ice floes on top of one another. The cubs discover one slab of ice that makes a perfect slide. While they toboggan down, their mother's strong sense of smell picks up the musky scent of ringed seals. She grunts to the cubs, urging them to pay attention. Playtime is over. Their first real lesson in survival is about to begin.

As the mother bear advances toward the smell, her head swings from side to side, her nose sniffing the air. Two arctic foxes follow the bears, hoping that they might scavenge on the mother's prey. Suddenly the mother stops and growls at the cubs to keep still. With a burst of speed, she races toward the hidden seals.

The mother bear raises her massive body and *THUMP!* She lands on the roof of the seals' birth lair with her heavy front legs.

The terrified mother seal pushes her pup through the *allu,* or breathing hole, into the water beneath the ice. Then she slips through the hole herself. *SMASH!* Pounding paws collapse the roof just as the seal's tail disappears. The mother bear tosses chunks of ice and snow to the side, but it is too late. The seals have fled to a safer place.

The bears continue their journey across the dangerous and ever-changing sea ice. Travel is often slow and tedious for the young cubs. Ice floes have crashed together in many places, creating *ivu*, or piles of upthrust ice. The female cub is struggling to keep up, when her paw suddenly breaks through a thin layer of snow. Her leg slips into a narrow crack and wedges tight between two walls of ice. In a panic, she cries for her mother.

The mother bear quickly returns. She grabs the cub in her mouth and pulls her gently from the crack. The other cub joins them. All three curl up for a nap in a safe spot behind a tower of stable ice.

The scent of a male polar bear awakens the mother. It is breeding season, a time when male bears will attack cubs. Alarmed, she softly growls at the cubs and hurries them away from the dangerous smell. In two years, when the cubs are on their own, she will be ready to mate again.

As the bears journey across the ice, the never-setting sun slowly circles the horizon. One May afternoon, the northern sky fills with billowing clouds. The wind shifts and blows hard from the south. The cubs hear the grinding, creaking, and smashing sounds of

moving ice. A gray streak of light stretches across the sky. Fast-moving ice has blown offshore, leaving an open lead of dark water, which is reflected in the clouds. The Inupiat call it *qisuk,* or water sky.

As they travel along the open lead, the mother bear sniffs a familiar musky smell. On a point of ice that juts out into the sea, a bearded seal rests in the sunshine while flocks of king eider ducks fly overhead.

The mother bear leaves the cubs where they can watch her stalk the seal. She slips quietly into the water, then paddles toward her prey. Her partially webbed toes and large front paws propel her, while her smaller hind feet help control her direction of travel. Her buoyant fat layer insulates her like a wetsuit.

Nearing the seal, she dives quietly underwater. Moments later, she explodes through the surface and onto the ice. She strikes the seal in the head with her paw, then bites the fragile skull with her long canine teeth. Within seconds, the seal is dead.

It is the first meal the mother bear has had in a long time. She eagerly devours all the skin, blubber, and meat. Although the cubs haven't begun to eat meat regularly, they lick the seal's remains and learn what their future meals will taste like. Two arctic foxes and some ivory gulls wait nearby to scavenge after the bears leave the site.

Summer days grow warmer, with temperatures in the thirties and forties. The cubs splash and frolic in shallow pools of melting sea ice.

The mother catches a whiff of a dead bear. If hungry, she might have scavenged on it. Luckily she leaves the carcass alone. The dead bear was poisoned from consuming a can of antifreeze, which it found near an industrialized area along the coast. When hungry

bears cannot catch seals, they will prey and scavenge upon anything in their path, including garbage and toxic substances. If the mother and cubs had scavenged on the bear, they could have become sick or died.

Increased development and global pollution are growing threats to polar bears and other animals of the Arctic. While the bears move on toward more open leads, a hungry arctic fox feeds upon the bear's carcass. It, too, may die from the poison.

As the sea ice continues to break up and drift offshore, the bears travel north to a large polynya, a water zone rich with marine life and free of ice. The mother decides that her eighty-pound cubs are ready for their first swimming lesson.

She plunges into the water and huffs at the cubs to follow. *Splash!* The female cub belly flops into the sea and paddles toward her mother. The second cub is a little tentative but jumps in so he's not left behind. The mother slowly swims in a circle.

The cub catches up, then grabs onto the mother's back for a ride.

A group of walrus watch them from a distance, and oldsquaw ducks dive beneath them. The cub slides off his mother's back. For the few moments his head is underwater, he hears the birdlike songs of bearded seals and beluga whales, and the deep voices of bowhead whales.

During August and September, the days grow shorter and cooler. Flocks of birds migrate south, flecking the clouds like dark pebbles scattered on a white cloth. As night returns, the north winds push grinding ice floes toward the shore.

The mother bear and her cubs have traveled hundreds of miles since leaving the den. Now they feel the change of season and move south with the windblown ice. One night, as the frozen sea locks itself to the shore, a new wonder appears. Waves of northern lights ripple and dance across the vast polar sky.

On a cold gray October day, the wind howls and snowflakes swirl around the cubs' faces. Waiting out the storm, the three bears curl up together. The snow covers their fur and protects them like a blanket. This is the first of many storms they will face this winter. With little open water, three months of darkness, and arctic blizzards, hunting will be difficult. The mother bear will still hunt, waiting patiently for seals to surface through their breathing holes.

By their first birthday, the cubs will have journeyed nearly fifteen hundred miles. With the coming spring, they will be strong enough to stalk and kill their own seals. Yet they will remain with their mother, the master hunter, for another year of training and protection. When she is ready to begin a new family, they will strike out on their own.

Until then, they will brave life on the top of the world together.

This book focuses on the Beaufort Sea polar bears, which live off the coast of northern Alaska and northwestern Canada. Approximately two thousand polar bears live in this region, out of a total world population of twenty to thirty thousand. The cubs in this story were born on the coast of the Arctic National Wildlife Refuge, an important denning area, where oil development has been proposed.

SCIENTIFIC NAME:
Ursus maritimus; means "bear of the sea"

INUPIAT ESKIMO NAMES:
Nanuq (nah-NOOK); means polar bear
Nanuayaag (nah-NOAH-yaak); means polar bear cubs

HEIGHT:
10 to 11 feet tall when standing on their hind legs, high enough to look an elephant in the eye

WEIGHT:
Males: average 1,000 pounds, about twice as heavy as a lion
Females: between 400 and 800 pounds
Cubs: 1 to 2 pounds at birth, about the size of a guinea pig

PHYSICAL DESCRIPTION:
Body: streamlined for swimming, with an angular head, small ears, and large canine teeth
Paws: the size of dinner plates, with webbed toes, bumpy pads to muffle noise and provide traction, and short, sharp claws for grabbing prey
Fur: a thick outer coat of transparent, water-repellent hairs, as well as a dense undercoat

HABITAT:
True marine mammals, they are the only bears that spend more time on the sea ice and in the water than on land. Females normally den every three years, on land or on the sea ice, producing one or two cubs.

FOOD:
Favorite: Seal blubber from ringed seals. One ringed seal will sustain a polar bear for about 11 days.
Other: Beluga whales, bearded seals, ducks, whale carcasses, walrus

A SPECIAL NOTE ON THE POLAR BEAR POPULATION AND ITS ENVIRONMENT:
Polar bears have few enemies besides killer whales, walrus, and human hunters. But because their reproduction rate is so low, they are a protected species. A 1973 international agreement signed by five nations prohibits hunting in denning areas, bans sport hunting, and allows subsistence hunting by Native peoples only. The Beaufort Sea bears are also protected under an agreement that prohibits the taking of females with cubs. Still, many people are concerned that the increases in global pollution and in oil and gas development in the Arctic will pose a great threat to the polar bears' environment—and so to the bears themselves.

JOURNEY OF THE BEARS

RUSSIA · CHUKCHI SEA · BEAUFORT SEA · DEN · ARCTIC REFUGE · CANADA · ALASKA

ALASKA SCIENCE CENTER, USGS

Text copyright © 1997 by Debbie S. Miller
Illustrations copyright © 1997 by Jon Van Zyle

First Edition

Library of Congress Cataloging-in-Publication Data

Miller, Debbie S.
    A polar bear journey / by Debbie S. Miller ; pictures by Jon Van Zyle.—1st ed.
        p.   cm.
    Summary: Details the life cycle of a mother polar bear and her two cubs, from their birth to their learning of survival lessons.
    ISBN 0-316-57244-6
    1. Polar bear—Arctic regions—Juvenile literature.
[1. Polar bear. 2. Bears.] I. Van Zyle, Jon, ill.
II. Title
QL737.C27M5 1997
599.74'446—dc20   96–42284

NIL 10 9 8 7 6 5 4 3 2

Published simultaneously in Canada by Little, Brown & Company (Canada) Limited

Printed in Italy

The paintings in this book were done in acrylic on untempered Masonite panels. The text was set in Albertus by Lasergraphics.